4-10

D0382981

DISCARD

Cowgirl Kate and Cocoa

Spring Babies

Cowgirl Kate and Cocoa

Spring Babies

Written by **Erica Silverman**

Painted by **Betsy Lewin**

Harcourt Children's Books ·
Houghton Mifflin Harcourt
Boston   New York   2010

To Allyn, Andrea, Sam, Betsy—
the best ranch crew ever!—E.S.

To Patty and Erica again, and to Dilys Evans.
It was a great ride.—B.L.

Text copyright © 2010 by Erica Silverman
Illustrations copyright © 2010 by Betsy Lewin

All rights reserved. For permission to reproduce selections from this book, write to
Permissions, Houghton Mifflin Harcourt Publishing Company, 215 Park Avenue South,
New York, New York 10003.

Harcourt Children's Books is an imprint of
Houghton Mifflin Harcourt Publishing Company.
www.hmhbooks.com

The illustrations in this book were done in watercolors
on Strathmore one-ply Bristol paper.
The display type was hand-lettered by Georgia Deaver.
The text type was set in Filosofia.

Library of Congress Cataloging-in-Publication Data
Silverman, Erica.
Cowgirl Kate and Cocoa : spring babies / by Erica Silverman ; painted by Betsy Lewin.
    p. cm.
Summary: Cowgirl Kate and her horse Cocoa watch over the new calves, a puppy, and some baby barn
owls.
  ISBN 978-0-15-205396-3
  [1. Animals—Infancy—Fiction. 2. Cowgirls—Fiction. 3. Horses—Fiction.] I. Lewin, Betsy, ill. II. Title.
  PZ7.S58625Cot 2010
  [E]—dc22   2009008399
Manufactured in Singapore
TWP 10 9 8 7 6 5 4 3 2 1
4500199785

Chapter 1

No More Calves!

"Cocoa, wake up," said Cowgirl Kate.

"We're going on night watch."

Cocoa opened his eyes.

He yawned.

"It's the middle of the night," he said.

"The cows should be sleeping."

"Tell that to the cows," said Cowgirl Kate.

"I would," said Cocoa, "but I don't want
to wake them up."

Cowgirl Kate put on Cocoa's saddle.
She led him outside.
"Cows sometimes have their calves at night,"
she said.

"No more calves!" cried Cocoa.

"They are too much work."

"Tell that to the cows," said Cowgirl Kate.

"I would," said Cocoa.

"But *that* would be too much work!"

Cowgirl Kate rode Cocoa to the spring pasture.

Mooo!

"That sounds like Sweety Pie," said Cocoa.

Moooooo!

"We have to find her!" said Cowgirl Kate.

Cowgirl Kate and Cocoa followed the sound of the mooing . . .

down a gully . . .

behind a bush.

"Sweety Pie!" cried Cowgirl Kate.

Sweety Pie walked around in circles.

She lay down.

She stood up.

She lay down again.

Moooooo! she moaned.

"Uh-oh!" cried Cocoa.

"I see a little calf head.

I see little calf hooves."

Cowgirl Kate grabbed her walkie-talkie.

"Mom! Dad!" she called.

"Come to the spring pasture!

Sweety Pie has started to calve!"

Cowgirl Kate slipped out of the saddle.

"Hold on, Sweety Pie," she said.

"Mom and Dad will be here soon."

"Too late!" said Cocoa.

"Look!"

A small wet calf was lying on the ground.
Sweety Pie licked him all over.
The calf opened his eyes.

He gazed at Sweety Pie.
He gazed at Cocoa.
He bobbed his head up and down.
Cocoa nickered.
"That little one needs us," he said.
"Let's stay and watch him until morning."

Cowgirl Kate smiled.

"Didn't you say calves are too much work?"
she asked.

"They *are* too much work," said Cocoa.

"And they are also sweet."
He leaned closer to Cowgirl Kate.

"But . . ." he whispered,

"I will *never* tell that to the cows!"

Chapter 2
Springy and Zingy

Whoosh! Cowgirl Kate tossed her rope at a calf.

The calf darted away.

"He sure is springy and zingy," said Cocoa.

"He's having fun," said Cowgirl Kate.

"I want to have fun, too," said Cocoa.

The calf kicked up his back hooves.

So did Cocoa.

"Whoa!" cried Cowgirl Kate.

The calf sprang straight up into the air.

So did Cocoa.

"Stop right now!" cried Cowgirl Kate.

"We have work to do!"

The calf jumped backwards.

So did Cocoa.

The calf darted and dashed.

Cocoa darted and—

Cowgirl Kate reached into her saddlebag.

CRUNCH!

Cocoa stopped.

He turned his head.

He stared.

"I want an apple, too!" he said.

"First, you must work," said Cowgirl Kate.

Cocoa grinned.

"I *was* working!" he said.

"You were jumping around like
a springy, zingy calf," Cowgirl Kate said.

"What kind of work is that?"

"Hard work. I was learning to think like
a springy, zingy calf," said Cocoa.
"It made me hungry!"
And he grabbed the apple.
CHOMP!

Chapter 3
A Present from Jenny

"Here comes Jenny!" said Cowgirl Kate.

"She's bringing us a present."

"Peppermint!" squealed Cocoa.

"Last time she brought peppermint candy."

"This will be better than peppermint,"
 said Cowgirl Kate.

"Nothing is better than peppermint!"
 said Cocoa.

Jenny got out of the car.

She was holding a puppy.

"Arf arf," barked the puppy.

"Cocoa, look!" cried Cowgirl Kate.

"Isn't the puppy cute?"

Cocoa snorted.

"What's wrong with Cocoa?" asked Jenny.

"I think he wanted peppermint candy,"

said Cowgirl Kate.

Cowgirl Kate and Jenny played fetch with
the puppy.
Cocoa snorted again.
They gave the puppy food and water.
Cocoa snorted again.
They made the puppy a cozy bed.
Cocoa stomped into the barn.

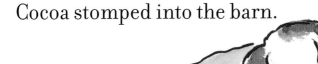

"I have to go," said Jenny.

"Thank you for my present!"
said Cowgirl Kate.

She carried the puppy into the barn.

"Cocoa," said Cowgirl Kate,

"Jenny gave this puppy to both of us."

"But I want peppermint," said Cocoa.

Cowgirl Kate put the puppy down.

The puppy bounced over to Cocoa.

"Arf arf," she barked.

"She's noisy," said Cocoa.

"She's talking to you," said Cowgirl Kate.

The puppy licked Cocoa's front legs.

"She's tickling me," said Cocoa.

"She likes you," said Cowgirl Kate.

The puppy blinked up at him.

"This puppy will help us herd cows,"
said Cowgirl Kate.

"Will she make my work easier?" asked Cocoa.

"Much easier," said Cowgirl Kate.

Cocoa leaned down.

His nose touched the puppy's nose.

"I am glad Jenny gave us this puppy," he said.

"And I know the perfect name for her."

"What?" asked Cowgirl Kate.

Cocoa grinned.

"Peppermint," he said.

Chapter 4
Ghost!

One night, Cocoa galloped out of the barn.
"Ghost!" he cried. "Ghost!"
Peppermint scrambled out after him.
"Arf!" she barked. "Arf!"

Cowgirl Kate came out of the house.

"Cocoa, what happened?" she asked.

"First I heard a spooky *hssssss*," said Cocoa.

"Arf!" barked Peppermint.

"And then a ghost floated over my head."

"Arf!" barked Peppermint.

"Let me see this ghost," said Cowgirl Kate.

She went into the barn and turned on the light.

Cocoa stood in the doorway.

He peered inside.

Peppermint hid behind Cocoa.

"Don't be scared," said Cowgirl Kate.

Cocoa snorted.

"I am not scared!" he said.

Hssssss.

"That's the ghost!" cried Cocoa.

"Arf!" barked Peppermint.

"That sound came from the loft,"
said Cowgirl Kate.

She climbed up the ladder.

"Oh, my!" she whispered.

"One, two, three, four, five," she counted.

"Five ghosts?" cried Cocoa.

"Five babies," said Cowgirl Kate.

"Five baby ghosts?" cried Cocoa.

"No," said Cowgirl Kate.

"Come see."

Cocoa put his front hooves on a bale of hay
and stretched out his neck.

"Those are not ghosts," he said.

"They're barn owls," whispered Cowgirl Kate.

"But what about the ghost that floated over
 my head?" asked Cocoa.
"That was their mama," said Cowgirl Kate.
"She flew outside to find food for her babies."

Hssssss, hissed the baby owls. *Hssssss*.

"What do they want?" asked Cocoa.

"They want their mama," said Cowgirl Kate.

Cocoa gazed at them.

"Your mama will come back," he said.

"But while she is out,

I will watch you."

"Arf!" barked Peppermint.

"Peppermint will watch you, too," said Cocoa.

"We will *all* be on night watch,"
said Cowgirl Kate.
"I love night watch," said Cocoa.
"And I love spring babies!"